The Nodland Express

First published in Great Britain 1995 by
Macmillan Children's Books
a division of Macmillan Publishers Limited
18-21 Cavaye Place, London SW10 9PG
and Basingstoke
Associated companies throughout the world

ISBN 0 333 61622 7 (hardback)
ISBN 0 333 61623 5 (paperback)

1 3 5 7 9 8 6 4 2

A CIP catalogue record for this book is available
from the British Library

Printed in Hong Kong

The Nodland Express

ANNA CLARKE

with illustrations by
MARTIN ROWSON

MACMILLAN CHILDREN'S BOOKS

For Fred and Rose

"Good night, Isaac,
good night Maude,"
called Mother.
"Off you go to
the Land of Nod!"
She closed the door.

"Isaac," said Maude in
the dark, "Mummy
always says that but
she never says
where it is or how
to get there. Do you
know?"
"What?"
"Do you know how
to get to the Land
of Nod?" said Maude.
"Oh . . . no, I don't,"
said Isaac,
"but I suppose you
could go any way
you like – by boat,
or plane, or car.
I know . . ."

". . . Let's go by train!"

Maude went to buy the tickets while
Isaac found out which train to catch.
"Two tickets for the Land of Nod, please."
"Is that a single or a return you want?"
asked the booking clerk.
"Oh! Return, of course," said Maude.
She could hear Isaac calling her to
hurry up.

"Look!" said Isaac. "Here's our train!"
They climbed on board just as the whistle was blown.

"All aboard the Nodland Express! Stand away!"
And the 19.30 Express to the Land of Nod pulled out of the station.

Maude and Isaac looked around
at the other passengers. Maude
put her mouth close to Isaac's ear
and said very quietly,
"Are you sure this is the right train?"

The witch was watching them whispering.
"What's the trouble, my tinies?" she asked,
spitting as she spoke. "Hungry? Here, have
a sandwich."
"No, thank you," said Isaac. "We're going
to the buffet car."

"Hey, Maude," said Isaac with his mouth full, "look out of the window! Isn't it fantastic!" Maude looked. "Isaac," she said, "are you absolutely sure this is the right train?"

When the children got back to their seats the wolf leaned across and said, "I say, could you two look after this bag for me? I've got too much luggage and they'll charge me excess, you know." He smiled and showed his teeth.

"Well . . ." said Maude.
". . . OK," said Isaac.

Nodland
Express
(Zzzzzzzz)

DO NOT THROW
PILLOWS OFF TRA

The train stopped. This was the border of the Land of Nod and inspectors and officials were getting on the train to check everyone's luggage and passports and tickets.

The Customs
Official came into
the compartment and
prodded some of the bags
and even opened one of them.
She was about to leave when she saw
the wolf's red bag under Maude's seat.
"Is that your bag?" she asked.
"No," said Maude.
The bag was dragged into the middle of the floor and the
Customs Official put her fingers on the clasp . . .

"No! Don't open it!" shrieked the wolf. "It's mine, the bag is mine! You mustn't open it here — it's full of nightmares!"

"It's my job to see that there are no nightmares in the Land of Nod," said the Customs Official. "This bag will be impounded and you, sir, *you* will travel no further on this train. Off you get!"

The witch had been rummaging in her cauldron. There was rubbish all over the floor but still she searched, muttering to herself, "If I do not find that spell, they will find *me* here as well! Rats!" Eventually she gave up and asked the walrus if she might borrow his newspaper. She was trying to hide behind it when a voice called "Passports! Please have your passports ready for inspection!"

The witch had made herself so small that Isaac and Maude thought she must have disappeared altogether.

But the officials found her all the same.
"Madam," said the Immigration Controller, "this passport is not valid in the Land of Nod. You must disembark here. I shall be confiscating your broomstick. Now come along and don't cause trouble." So the witch had to get off.

The toad was next. The Ticket Inspector asked for his ticket. The toad gave him a rather chewed and dirty piece of paper which the inspector held by its corner and looked at carefully.

"I am afraid, Mr . . . er . . . Toad, that this is an Afternoon Snooze Ticket. It is not valid on the Nodland Express. You must change here and wait for tomorrow's Slow Train To Teatime. Go on, hop it!" So the toad had to get off, too.

Maude and Isaac need not have worried. There was nothing wrong with their tickets or passports. Their luggage was in order, too.

"One bear, one penguin – yes, that's all in order and no duty to pay, thank you," said the Customs Official.

"Two child returns to the Land of Nod. Thank you, that'll do nicely," said the Ticket Inspector.

"Children on the Nodland Express do not require passports – it says so here in my book of regulations, number 302 subsection six," said the Immigration Controller.

Isaac and Maude sat
back in their seats,
happy to enjoy the
rest of their journey.
But as it grew darker
outside they began
to wonder if the
Nodland Express
would ever reach its
destination.

"Oh Isaac," said Maude,
"are we nearly there?
I'm so tired!"
"It's all right, I can see
the Land of Nod in
the distance."

The train pulled into
the station.
"Nodland Central!
This train will terminate
here! All change!"
shouted the Guard.
Isaac and Maude got
down onto the platform
and looked around.
Someone was calling
their names.

"Maude and Isaac, welcome to the Land of Nod! Please follow me. You will be spending the night at the Nodland Grand Terminus Hotel." The Station Manager smiled at them briskly and said, "Oh but you're very sleepy, aren't you? Come along, let's just make sure you've got everything you require and then get you tucked up in bed." Maude and Isaac looked at him and smiled.

"This way,
Isaac, this way,
Maude," said the Hotel
Manager. "The porters will
carry your luggage.
Keep your eyes open just a little longer
and you won't trip over that sleeping hippo.
You'd like to go to bed, wouldn't you?"
The children nodded.
"Here's your room. I'll just tuck you up."

"Good night, Isaac.
Good night, Maude."

Other Macmillan picture books you will enjoy